# JACK AND THE BEANSTALK

## and Other Favorite Folk Tales

# Editor's Note

The stories in this book,
    Jack and the Beanstalk,
    Rumpelstiltskin,
    and The Elves and the Shoemaker,
have been among children's favorite folk tales
for hundreds of years. Jack and the Beanstalk was
well-known before 1807, when it was printed in a series
called "Popular Stories." Rumpelstiltskin and The Elves
and the Shoemaker were collected by the Brothers Grimm
in the early 1800s.
    In each of these stories, a magical creature helps the hero
find fortune. But while Jack must steal it from the giant,
and Rumpelstiltskin will only help the miller's daughter for
a price, the elves bring it freely to the honest shoemaker and
are rewarded in turn.

# JACK AND THE BEANSTALK
## and Other
## Favorite Folk Tales

Illustrated by Richard Walz

A GOLDEN BOOK • NEW YORK
Western Publishing Company, Inc., Racine, Wisconsin 53404

# Jack and the Beanstalk

ONCE UPON A TIME there lived a poor widow with her son Jack.

Jack was a good-natured boy, but too lazy to earn a living. Soon they had nothing left in the world but a leaky hut and an old cow.

"Jack," said his mother one day, "we haven't a penny for food. You must take the cow to market and sell her."

The sun was warm overhead when Jack started down the road toward town, with the old cow bobbing along behind him.

He hadn't gone far when suddenly, out of a cloud of dust, a strange little man appeared.

"Son," said the little man, "that's a pretty cow. Where are you leading her?"

"To market to sell her," said Jack.

"I'll give you these for your cow," said the man, opening his hand. There in his palm lay the prettiest red and yellow and blue beans that Jack had ever seen. The more Jack looked at the beans, the more he wanted them.

"It's a bargain," said he, and he took the beans. As the old man led the cow away, Jack patted her for the last time and started for home.

"Mother, see what I got for the cow," he cried as he flung open the door.

"A handful of beans!" she wept angrily. She tossed the beans out the window. "Now we can have no supper!"

It was a hungry Jack who sobbed himself to sleep that night.

But when he awoke the next morning, a strange sight sent him leaping out of bed to the window. Leaves the size of elephants' ears shaded his room! "That's odd!" he exclaimed. "They weren't there last night!"

He hurried outdoors. There was a tall green beanstalk reaching far, far up in the sky. It had grown from the beans.

"It must have a top," thought Jack, staring upward till his neck was stiff. "I'll climb till I reach it."

And up, up, up the beanstalk he climbed, till the hut below was nothing but a black speck.

At last the beanstalk ended on top of a cloud. Jack saw a tremendous stone castle.

He found his way into the castle. After wandering
through its echoing halls he entered the great kitchen,
where the kind old cook was removing a pan of bread
from the oven. When she saw Jack, she dropped the pan
with a clatter.

"Don't you know that a vicious giant owns this castle?
He eats boys like you," she warned.

Suddenly the floor shook and the walls trembled.

"Here he comes!" whispered the cook. "Hide!"

Just as Jack climbed into the cupboard, a fierce giant, about four stories high, stamped into the room.

"Fee, fi, fo, fum, I smell the blood of an Englishman," he roared, swinging his club. He sniffed in all the corners. He sniffed under his big chair. He sniffed near the cupboard.

" 'Tis nothing but roast pork," quavered the old cook, setting a huge steaming platter on the table.

"Roast pork!" said the giant. It was his favorite dish! To Jack's relief, he fell to eating at once.

Jack hungrily watched the giant gobble down enough dinner for twenty.

Then the giant called for his magic hen. The cook
brought it.

"Lay a golden egg!" the giant roared, and in a twinkling,
a golden egg shone on the table.

"That's a handy hen to own," thought Jack.

And when at last the giant's head nodded in a snooze,
Jack slipped out of the cupboard, quietly tucked the hen
under his arm, and fled down the beanstalk to his home.

In no time at all the magic hen made Jack and his
mother rich.

The weeks flew by. Then one summer day Jack decided
to climb the beanstalk again. Once more he stole into the
giant's castle.

This time when the giant's footsteps shook the castle,
Jack hid under the table.

The giant sniffed about in the corners.

"Fee, fi, fo, fum, I smell the blood of an Englishman," he roared.

"'Tis roast goose," said the cook, and again the giant sat down to his dinner. He then counted his gold and fell asleep.

While the giant was napping, Jack ran off with two bags of gold, and arrived home safely.

The third time Jack went to the castle, the giant had his dinner and then called for his magic harp. When he fell asleep, Jack crept stealthily out of the cupboard, snatched the harp, and ran for the distant beanstalk.

But the magic harp began to tinkle a tune. Back in the kitchen the giant awakened with a grunt that shook the castle.

"Fee, fi, fo, fum, I smell the blood of an Englishman!"
he thundered. "And this time I'll catch him!"

He ran out of the castle after Jack.

"Catch me if you can," shouted Jack, reaching the
beanstalk. Then down the beanstalk he hustled, with the
giant close behind him.

Down, down, down he climbed, in the shadow of the giant. He had to hold on tight, for the beanstalk trembled and shook under the giant's weight.

Closer and closer and closer came the giant, till his breath was a powerful wind that almost blew Jack away. Jack heard his mother scream.

"Mother, Mother," he called, "get me the ax from the shed!"

At last Jack slid to the ground. Snatching the ax from his mother, he chopped the beanstalk through.

Down fell the beanstalk to the earth, and down, down fell the giant. He crashed to the ground below, burying himself deep in the earth. And that was the end of the giant.

But Jack and his mother, wealthy with the riches Jack had brought from the castle, lived happily ever after.

# Rumpelstiltskin

THERE ONCE LIVED a miller who was so proud of his daughter's beauty that he wanted to tell everyone about it.

One day the miller saw the King and his men out hunting in the forest. Now the King was young and handsome, and the miller told him about his beautiful daughter.

"Sire," he said, bowing low, "I have a daughter. Not only is she beautiful, but she can also spin straw into gold."

"Bring her to me at once," said the King. For though he was a king, he was not very rich, and he needed gold.

The King was delighted when he saw that the miller's daughter was indeed very beautiful. But he remembered what the miller had said, and he ordered her to spin a roomful of straw into gold.

The boastful miller was to be held a prisoner until the King had all the gold he needed.

The miller's daughter had never in her life spun straw into gold, nor did she know how it was done. She looked at the straw, and she looked at the spinning wheel, and she thought of her father, and she burst into tears.

"Why do you weep, mistress miller?" said a voice. The girl saw a tiny little man. Ugly he was, but with a twinkle in his eye, and the girl told him of her plight.

"Hmmm," said the little man. "Spin straw into gold. What will you give me if I do it for you?"

"My necklace," said the girl at once. It was the most precious thing she owned.

Then *whirr-whirr*, the little man started the spinning wheel, and *whirr-whirr* it went all night, spinning the straw into precious gold.

The King was so delighted when he saw all the gold next morning that he decided he must have some more. And once again, the little man appeared to help the miller's daughter. She gave him her ring, and *whirr-whirr*, he spun the straw into precious gold.

"Oh, miller's daughter," said the King next morning, "not only are you the most beautiful girl in the world, but you are also the cleverest. If you will spin me one more cartload of gold, you shall be my wife."

Now the girl was very pleased that the King wanted to marry her, for she thought him exceedingly handsome. But how could she pay the little man this time? She had already given him her necklace and her ring. "I have nothing left to give!" she wailed when the little man appeared.

And the little man said, "If you will promise to give me your first child, I will do it for you."

The poor girl agreed, and *whirr-whirr*, the little man
started the spinning wheel, and *whirr-whirr* it went all
night, spinning the straw into precious gold.

The King was overcome with delight when he saw the
gold shining in the morning sunlight, and the miller's
daughter beside it, even more beautiful than the gold.

He ordered the marriage ceremony to begin at once, and
the miller to be set free. And that is how the miller's
daughter became a queen.

In a year's time, the young Queen gave birth to a beautiful baby daughter. All the people in the land rejoiced when they heard of the birth of a princess. There was singing and dancing in the streets, and all the houses were covered with flowers and flags.

But none were more pleased than the happy King and Queen.

One day, as the Queen sat holding her baby, she heard a chuckle behind her. She turned, and saw the same little man who had helped her spin the straw into gold.

"I have come for your baby," he said. "You promised that you would give her to me."

Oh, how the Queen wept and pleaded with the little
man! She offered him money and costly jewels and a
splendid position at court. But he shook his head.

"No, a baby is far more precious than any of these
things," he said. "But I will give you one chance. Tell me,
within three days, what my name is. If you can guess right,
you shall keep the baby and never see me again."

And with that he disappeared.

The next day he was back again, and the Queen said all the names she could think of. But the little man just shook his head, and went away chuckling.

The next day the Queen sent messengers throughout the kingdom to find the names of all the people. She said them to the little man when he came.

But the little man just shook his head, and went away chuckling.

On the third day, one of the messengers came to the Queen and said, "I came to a high mountain at the end of the forest, and there I saw a little house. Before the house a fire was burning, and round the fire a little man was jumping. An ugly little man he was, but with a twinkle in his eye, and he was saying these words:

"'Today I brew, tomorrow I bake,
The next day the Queen's child I take.
For the Queen can never guess my fame—
That Rumpelstiltskin is my name.'"

As soon as the Queen heard these words, she knew that she was saved. She rewarded the messenger handsomely, and sat down to await the little man, her baby on her knee.

The little man appeared, and the Queen began to say more names to him—Harry and Parry and Williamsey-Morrisey and Peterkin-Hopewell-Jones. But it was none of these, as the Queen well knew, and the little man held out his arms for the baby.

The Queen began to rock her baby to and fro, then she said, "Why, then, perhaps your name is—could it be—I think it must be—Rumpelstiltskin!"

Oh, how angry that little man was! "Someone told you! Someone told you!" he screamed in a rage. He tore at his hair and he jumped and he groaned, and then he started to stamp his feet in a very, very angry way.

And, do you know, he stamped so hard he stamped himself right through the floor. And he has not been seen again, from that day to this.

And so the King and the Queen and their little daughter—and, of course, the miller, too—all lived happily ever after.

# The Elves and the Shoemaker

ONCE UPON A TIME a shoemaker and his wife lived together in great poverty. Although he worked hard and was honest, the shoemaker grew poorer and poorer, until one day there was only enough money left to buy leather for one pair of shoes. The shoemaker worked carefully on this leather, and just before he went to bed he finished cutting it so he could start to sew the first thing the next morning.

In the morning the shoemaker went into his shop, all ready to work, and there, on his workbench, stood the shoes—all finished! They were of perfect workmanship, finely and neatly made. The shoemaker and his wife, who came in when she heard his cries of amazement, were puzzled, and could not imagine who had done this for them.

That day a customer came in, and when he saw the beautiful shoes he bought them immediately, paying a very high price. With this money, the shoemaker bought enough leather for two pairs of shoes, and cut them out before he went to bed.

The next morning, what was the shoemaker's surprise to find two pairs of shoes all finished on his workbench! Again they were carefully and neatly made. He could not imagine who had done such fine work. Shortly after, two customers came in and bought the two pairs of shoes, and paid a very high price for them.

With this money, the shoemaker bought enough leather to make four pairs of shoes. That night, before he went to bed, he cut the shoes out and left them on his workbench. And the next morning when he came in, there were four pairs of shoes! By this time the shoemaker was completely astounded.

This went on for a long time. Whatever the shoemaker cut out in the evening was all finished in the morning, and the workmanship was so good that he sold all the shoes at a high price. He soon became prosperous again, and he and his wife were very happy.

When Christmastime was near, the shoemaker's wife said, "Let us hide tonight and watch. Perhaps we can find out who is being so kind to us."

So that night they hid behind some curtains and quietly watched. At midnight they heard scurrying footsteps, and what was their surprise to see two little elves who had not a stitch of clothing on!

The little men set to work industriously, stitching and rapping and tapping at such a great rate that the shoemaker could hardly follow the movements of their hands. They worked without stopping for a second until all the night's work was done, then scurried off into the darkness as quick as a flash. The shoemaker and his wife were so amazed they could do nothing but stare at each other.

The next morning, however, the wife said, "I have been thinking about those good little elves who have been so kind to us. They have made us wealthy, and I think we should do something for them in return. Since tonight is Christmas Eve, let us give them a present."

The shoemaker agreed to this, so they set to work, and the wife made two little sets of clothing—caps, trousers, and shirts. And the shoemaker made two tiny pairs of shoes. That evening, they laid the tiny wardrobes on the workbench and hid behind the curtain to watch.

At midnight the two little elves came in and went busily to the workbench. They gasped when they saw the tiny clothes. But they quickly dressed themselves, and they danced and jumped about as happy as could be. Then, suddenly, with merry laughs, they ran out the door, across the street, and out of sight.

The shoemaker and his wife never saw them again, nor did they ever come back to work at the shoemaker's bench. But the shoemaker and his wife were happy and successful from that time on as long as they lived.